Eraser Ark

Steven Bazydlo

Copyright/ Trademark

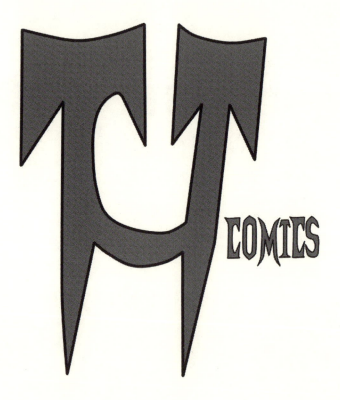

This story is a work of fiction. Names, characters, places, and
incidents are either products of the author's imagination or
used fictitiously. Any resemblance to actual events, locales,
or persons, living or dead, is entirely coincidental.
All rights reserved.
No part of this publication can be reproduced or transmitted
in any form or by any means, electronic or mechanical,
without permission in writing TcTComics or from Steven Bazydlo.

TcTcomics – Publisher

Scott Dyson – Editor

Lemseh Carother-Abdullah – Book Jacket

Steven Bazydlo – Author and Cover Artist

File 0- Code Name "Discovery"

Walking into the office, I couldn't help but remember how many missions had been carried out from this very room.

I opened the cabinet behind the desk and there they were: a file I hadn't looked at in years and a bottle of whiskey. I knew this was going to be a rough read if I ever chose to look back at it, but given the circumstances I thought a drink and a read-through might be needed to keep a record.

"File-000" It was a copy I kept in order to always remember where it all started.

Watching the clock tick by second by second was mind numbing. Day in and day out, never knowing when the timer would eventually hit zero for the final time.

I felt the feeling of dread as I pulled out the specialized recorder, an emotion I'd lost any hope of ever feeling again, given some of the close calls I'd witnessed. I poured myself a shot of the caramel-colored liquid and grimaced at the sudden burn in my throat as I threw it back.

"Well, better get started."

Pressing the record button, I heard the oddly satisfying click and sighed as if a huge weight had started to lift. *How do I even start this?* I watched the steady line of the recorder rise and fall very slightly with the subtle background noise of my breathing.

"Hello. The following recordings will be used to hopefully inform whoever comes after of what to prepare for. In this room you will find a chronicle of everything we have uncovered regarding the facilities that are assumed to be the only places that will survive this cataclysmic event.

"Where I work can only be explained as a nightmare. My job consists of me watching these timers as they count down and eventually release unholy horrors that will pose a significant threat to the human race. The organization I work for doesn't have a name, yet they have all the funding needed to bankroll this entire operation. However, all the missions and all the best efforts we made seem all for naught at the current time, given what is happening to our moon.

"I think that these recordings and files I am locking into our so called "time capsule" will help whoever or whatever evolves next.

"If and when you uncover this… sarcophagus of information, please, I beg of you not to think that this is some kind of elaborate prank or the ramblings of a drunken madman... well I might be a little drunk but I assure you that I am not crazy.

"What we uncovered and what we did to safeguard the world as a whole, going so far as to orchestrate wars and the deaths of countless innocents for the greater good, this all was done so the people would not have to know of the horrible fate that was in store for us all if we hadn't performed these absolutely necessary evils. What has escaped cannot be stopped. It is like some computer decided to hit some kind of human restart button and much like the computer, we were powerless to stop it. Even if we could, the damage done would end us in a matter of months, maybe a year or two if we were lucky."

Lighting up a cigarette, I let the ashy smoke slowly soothe me a little more before I continued. I knew I was running out of time and had to get to the point of the matter.

"These... creatures are impossibly ancient by our standards. I pray that what happens now may end this hellish cycle; however, with all we know now, it is entirely possible that even though we will be gone, the places I am referencing will inevitably survive us like all the other times.

"Simply saying this out loud is surreal. It's not even just that the structures themselves are damn near indestructible, it is the creatures that they house are on a whole other level of evolution. They have incredible strength and would give even horror movies a run for their money. In fact, when there was a leak of one of our footage files, we ended up spinning a P.R. campaign that turned into an online short film that eventually spawned a brand-new genre of survival horror-based games and movies. If only the general population knew the truth."

I sighed, took another shot and dragged another hit from my almost finished smoke. The heavy weight of the responsibility of what I was doing now started to really set in. I continued to talk into the recording device.

"What the average person of the world refers to as monsters in history and myth, were actually just instances of escaped creatures, or possibly scouts activated by the region's corresponding Facility to feel out where the planet stood on an evolutionary standpoint.

"The types of things that I now am in charge of and the facility that we work out of still perplexed us, as it was shown to have been around since the beginning of the Earth's Precambrian era, if not even earlier in time. It seems that this was one of the newer additions. We don't know where it came from; however, the technology in it is far beyond what modern science could ever hope to achieve in the next thousand years. I mean we had our theories, but the reality is far more difficult to understand. I will get to that in the later reports.

"Sorry I'm getting side tracked."

I paused as the countdown announcement interrupted me.

"Time until impact, T minus seven hours"

I shuddered. *Only seven hours…*

"Apologies, the automated system is only doing its job of letting me know how long before I am the last living thing on the planet."

I closed my eyes and rubbed my temples and thought about what to say next into the recording device.

"To better explain how I ended up here, I should go back to where it all began."

~

When I was a young fresh out of college research student, I was always open to whatever project was given to me until I could find my niche in the scientific community. My major of choice was cryptozoology, and I also added a double minor in ancient technology and mythology.

Yes, I know now that it was very weird to have that class load, however I was a young kid still obsessed with the thought of discovering Bigfoot or that chupathingy down in Mexico. If I knew then what I know now, I would have just become an accountant or something menial, because I think in this situation, ignorance would have been bliss.

Given my areas of expertise, I wasn't really on many lists for people to hire. I was hovering between UFO conspiracy theorists and the people who hunt Bigfoot on TV while doing horrible product placement. So needless to say, I was more or less doing my major as a part-time gig while working at a number of dead-end jobs to pay rent. The day that all changed, I was sitting on my couch in my underwear after having worked a double and just not feeling like wearing clothes. I was searching a job-finder website when a notification popped up in my email.

It seemed like just a generic email:

"Dear Mr. So and so, we came across your resume and would like to offer you a job opportunity."

I almost laughed it off as the company name was clearly made up. A search online came up with no background other than a picture of a small office in front of some strip mall in the middle of nowhere. I was bored and this was clearly a scam, so I decided if they were going to waste my time I might as well have some fun and waste theirs.

"Dear nameless company, I am very interested in what your job has to offer. What is the position you are offering and what is the salary?"

I hit the send button and, as I was closing the laptop, I heard a *ping* sound notifying me that I had another email. I paused for a second and opened it up to see that I received a message from an email address that appeared almost randomly typed. It was from the same company.

"Thank you for your reply. You have ten minutes before a car will be at your residence to retrieve you. Please pack a bag to be gone for at least a week. All questions will be answered upon your arrival at the airport."

What the hell is this? Closing my laptop, I laughed at the absurdity of whatever they were trying to scam me for. I plopped my wedgied ass back on my couch to finish whatever show I happened to be tuned into at the time.

My address wasn't even on the resume' and besides the nearest airport was currently shut down due to a pandemic.

A few minutes must have passed watching some videos when I heard my doorbell ring. checked the time. Roughly ten minutes had passed since I'd received that strange reply.

"No... no way that was a legit offer." I stood up and stared at my door.

Again my doorbell rang, followed up by a gentle knock.

Walking over to the door, I cracked it open hiding my lack of clothes behind it. A tall man wearing a suit was standing outside.

"Hello?" I asked, slightly confused. "Can I help you?" I was admittedly a little terrified at what the response might be.

The man stood straight as he asked me my name and whether I was ready to go.

Not knowing what to say, I simply tried to explain to him I thought that the offer was a joke or a scam given just how weird the way it was written.

He scowled and shook his head. He said, "We get that reaction a lot, but if you're coming with me, we have very little time. The plane is waiting." He was understanding. However, he informed me that I was going with him, that there wasn't any time for joking around and that the plane was already waiting.

I was stunned about how this guy seemed so matter of fact in his conviction that this was an actual job and that I apparently was hired sight unseen and without any interview. I hadn't realized the door had opened and I saw the eyes give me a once over in a clearly judgmental way.

He sighed. "I see you may need a few minutes to get ready. I'll notify the pilot, but please hurry; our employer does not like to be kept waiting and given he has shown interest in you, it would be in your best interest to accept the offer he has given."

Could this guy be serious? I mean, I am barely qualified to even write a paper for review. What possibly could be the assignment? I was both intrigued and scared at the notion, but felt compelled at this point to at least humor the benefactor since this didn't appear to be a joke.

Packing my bags, a number of questions ran through my head. I couldn't understand why my resume would draw any kind of attention other than some piddly-ass research group. But judging by the car and the nice suit the driver was wearing, I thought that this might be just what I need for a big break.

If only I'd seen those the gleaming red flags for what they were. I guess hindsight truly is twenty-twenty.

We made the drive to the airport in almost complete silence. Well, not on my part. I asked question after question, but the only response I was given was "you will understand when on the plane."

"The car bypassed the public entrance to the airport. Instead, we passed through a gate I'd never noticed before and finally drove to a fenced-in area behind the terminals, directly onto the tarmac where a small private jet stood ready for us.

I stumbled up the stairs with my suitcase. At the plane's entrance, I was greeted by a very well-dressed assistant who asked my name. She checked something off on a clipboard before leading me to a seat past a very attractive female and a very annoyed looking man. I didn't recognize either of them. I assumed the man was some sort of security officer, given that he had a weapons case next to him. The woman seemed to be in a similar confused state as I was; she was surrounded by several old-looking books and journals. *Clearly another researcher.*

~

I sighed and took another shot. "I miss those two."

~

Before I could ask any questions the door to the ramp was closed and the assistant with the clipboard addressed us from the front of the cabin.

"Thank you for accepting our employer's offer. The three of you will all be assigned a pseudonym as this is a somewhat secret assignment. You have all been chosen according to your strengths in certain fields that have been flagged as needed.

"Ma'am, you are to be referred to and respond to the name Ms. T. You sir," she pointed to the other man, "as a security officer, you will, from this point, be referred to as Mr. J.

She looked right at me and said, "And as for the cryptozoologist, you will be called Mr. D." I nodded, not really understanding what the purpose of these new monikers was.

"Pardon me." Raising my hand. "Why can't we use our regular names? I mean, what are we even doing here in the first place?"

"Oi mate, I've been on this plane for hours now and still don't know what the fuck is going on. All I was told was to bring what I felt would be suited for "big game" and I plan on killing something." The man we were to refer to as "Mr. J" seemed to have a heavy Australian accent and gave off a bit of an asshole vibe. Ms. T chimed in, her accent suggesting a Scandinavian origin, possibly Swedish. "Relax, sir. You are not the only one who has been kept in the dark.

The assistant took an exasperated breath before speaking. It made me think that this had been Mr. J's general attitude the whole time.

"As I was saying. Now that you are all here, I am at liberty to explain what our project is, and what your collective knowledge has to offer.

About a year ago, while drilling for mineral deposits, one of our teams discovered a large metallic structure about a mile down. So large, in fact, that it would make a modern-day skyscraper. look like an ant hill as compared to a mountain."

"Sounds to me like you need archaeologists, mate, not a guy with a gun." The cocky tone in Mr. J's voice was just oozing with douchbaggery.

Though she was obviously annoyed at this point, the assistant continued. "A research team was sent down into the shaft and discovered that there was another tunnel leading away from the structure towards a large door. After some considerations, the door was pried open. Behind it was a man-made cave system. All the walls of the cave were engraved in great detail using a pictorial language that appeared to describe the structure as an ark of some sort. However, some of the pictures have eroded over time. Samples were sent and they came back as an outcrop of bedrock. So whoever – or whatever –built this subterranean structure had to have either built it during the early stages of earth or had to have built it farther back than even before modern *homo sapiens* walked the earth. The implications of this discovery are world-changing.

"The reason that you, sir, and Mr. D are being hired is due to the fact that whatever is *in* the structure, according to the engravings, appears to be something currently unknown to man.

"The more concerning part is that the few effective scans we have been able to make suggest that it isn't empty and that it possibly is acting as its own terrarium of sorts."

Mr. J. guffawed. "Alright lady, you picked us up and you are talking about aliens? You're off your fucking rocker if you expect us to believe that."

"Seriously?" Ms. T asked. "Do you really think that it might contain some sort of aliens?"

"Well not necessarily aliens; however, at this point we are not ruling out the prospect."

The sound of their voices was drowned out by the thoughts in my own head. To me, this was a huge discovery and exactly what I have been waiting for my whole life. I felt my excitement rising within me. What an opportunity!

But what kind of creatures were we going to find? Billions of years of evolution with no clue as to what the base life form was meant that we could be looking at something created from a whole new branch of the evolutionary tree.

This begged the question: Why were they not using more established individuals? I mean, I felt honored to be a part of this history making moment: however, I still had that question nagging at me in the back of my head.

"You were all chosen for various reasons; however, our benefactor wanted to give a ... younger generation an opportunity to make a name for themselves. Also, to answer your remark Ms. T will be our resident archaeologist, Mr. J. Does that suffice for you?"

An awkward silence fell between the two, as Ms. T and I smiled at the amount of sass that was so elegantly worded towards the smart-ass. It was almost like there was now a playful sexual tension between the two.

The assistant walked, soldier-like, through the cabin toward the back of the aircraft. She passed through a door and disappeared into a private compartment. We felt the acceleration as the plane started its takeoff.

Mr. J turned to us. "Ah, that bitch is a few stubbies short of a six pack, I'd wager. The fuck she goin' on about aliens?"

"Well given the relative age of the rock, the chances it was built by anything human is very slim."

"It's a load of bollocks." The angry man waved us away as he turned to the window and watched the tarmac rush by.

I felt my stomach sink as we rose up into the air, finally settling when we reached altitude. Ms. T sat quietly in her own little world typing away at whatever she was doing and Mr. J sat still fuming and watched the clouds through his little window.

Taking out my phone, I tried to watch some videos, but the Wi-Fi was being blocked and even its data was jammed. Whoever was financing this really didn't want us contacting anyone about where we were going, wherever that might be. I thought about getting up and going back to knock on that little door but in the end, I stayed put. At some point I must have fallen asleep.

I woke up to the bright light of the sun shining through my little window, the wing of the plane blocking most of my view. The others were still asleep and the assistant was nowhere to be seen. I wondered if they might have introduced something into the cabin's air to relax us.

A crackly male voice came over an intercom informing us that we were beginning our approach and that we were to remain seated. I felt our descent mildly, as it was causing a slight rise in my stomach. The view changed from mostly blue sky for me to a seemingly endless desert.

I heard a noise next to me and looked over to see Ms. T beginning to pack up her materials. She must have woken up during the message. Mr. J. was still asleep as far as I could tell, but when I felt the tires hit the landing strip, the bounce jostled him awake. "For fuck's sake mate, give us a little warning before landing." No one paid any attention to him, as far as I could tell.

When we came to a stop, the assistant appeared from the cockpit area. She gestured for us to rise, collect our belongings, and head to the door.

The heat that met us was a significant change from where I was just a few hours before. As I stepped out onto the stairs, I could feel the cool air rushing out of the parked aircraft behind me. For just a second, I thought of turning around and going right back into that plane.,

A white SUV was parked at the base of the stairs; a large Arabic man stood by the open rear door of the vehicle.

"Where are we?" Mr. J. asked from behind me.

The assistant stood at the opening into the plane and said with a smile, "Welcome to Iraq."

"Are you fucking bonkers lady? This place is a bloody war zone!"

"I assure you; you will be fine. The local royalty has been paid a hefty sum in order to give us safe passage, as well as guaranteeing the security for our camp. However, at this time I must ask you to please join our large friend in the SUV, as I have someplace else I have to be."

"What? You got a hot date there love?"

"Not that it is any of your business, Mr. J., but I do more than just deliver people such as yourself around the world. Now as entertaining as this conversation is and has been with you, I must be on my way. Due to Mr. D. being late, my schedule has been changed. So please, do have a good day."

She turned to go back into the jet. I spoke up quickly before she could close the door. "Wait, why are we in Iraq?" I asked, confused on just how long I had to have been asleep in order to travel this far.

"Why? This is the cradle of civilization. You will be given more information on your objective upon arrival at the camp. Now if you will, I must depart."

With that she closed the door. We swiftly descended the stairs as the plane's engines began to rev. As we reached the SUV, the stairs rolled away and the plane began to taxi.

"Oi mate, I think she likes me."

"Um... Yeah sure she does." I saw Ms. T. roll her eyes. Maybe Mr. J. saw it, too.

"What do you think there, sweety?"

"I do not care. We are on an expedition that could change the world and you can't get the thought of sex out of your head."

"What can I say, I'm a charma."

"I think you will have a new name for me."

"Is that right? Well, what is it, my dear? I'm all ears."

"I think I shall call you *skitstovel*."

"Oh I like that! It sounds sexy."

"You go ahead and think that."

The look on Mr. J's face went from a shit-eating grin to confusion before noticing I was looking at him, a smile apparently on my face.

"What you laughing at, ya little prick? About fucking face and walk!" he said, shoving my shoulder.

The trip into the desert was quiet. Our chauffeur didn't speak English, or if he did, he didn't want to show it. This became more evident as Mr. J. kept asking him stupid questions or making racial jokes. Ms. T. kept busy, but from time to time would look up in disgust at the comments she was hearing. I was curious as to what she was working on though.

"Sorry... Pardon me, but what are you working on?"

She seemed to be using the same plan as the driver and ignored my question.

"Excuse me? Ms. T.?"

Looking up from her computer like an angry librarian, she looked down and back towards me.

"Sorry," I apologized. "I'm just curious and seeing as our Mr. J. is busy, I wanted to get to know you."

"I am busy with real work; I'm currently preparing a paper for review."

"What's that supposed to mean? I'm just curious about your work."

"Sorry, I have been stuck on that plane with that *skitstovel* for an unbearable number of hours. He made an extremely rude comment, and when I didn't respond to it as he wanted, it resulted in me slapping him. The assistant whispered something to him that made him even madder, if that was possible."

She kept referring to Mr. J. with that word and I needed to know what it meant.

"What does that mean?"

"I do not know what she said; however. he seems to have no manners."

"No, I mean what does that word mean?"

She chuckled before leaning in and whispering, "In English, it means something close to a boot filled with fecal matter. Only not as censored." A small smile finally appeared on her face, distracting from her otherwise very serious demeanor.

I couldn't help but laugh at the translation.

The rest of the trip was uneventful. Ms. T. explained to me what her paper was about and it seemed pretty out there. I didn't understand most of it; however, it basically boiled down to how there were several places of worship around the world that all had similarities to Stonehenge, several of which seemed to line up. Her paper suggested that if we were to dig under these sites, we might find hidden libraries of ancient knowledge. It was a very out-of-the-ordinary topic; however, I was impressed by her logic and her assumptions. She had tons of pictures of artifacts and places from all around the world suggesting that these libraries existed. I found her arguments to be quite compelling, to say the least.

As we talked, I learned that she received the same message I did, and there had been a photo attached to the message. The photo showed the camp and a large hole that was next to a series of concentric circles of black stone. She tried to download it; however, when she made the attempt, the image deleted itself as someone knocked on her door.

And, well here she was, now. Here we all are.

When we finally arrived, she fell silent and my heart skipped a beat. What we saw as we crested a dune was almost an exact replica of Stonehenge. The only difference that I could see was that these gigantic stone pillars were black as coal. Tent-like buildings were surrounding the area with obviously armed guards patrolling it.

"The bloody hell is that?"

"That is a marked site. Who knows what knowledge lies beneath it," the Ms.T.'s angelic voice chimed in.

"Hopefully I can finally get a bloody drink. This heat is even too hot for me."

"Will you please just shut your mouth!"

"Seems like you got a spider up your arse, lady."

"You are that spider, *skitstovel*," she said under her breath. I chuckled.

We felt the SUV slow to a stop, Mr. J. and Ms. T. were still bickering when I left the vehicle. I was so entranced by the dig site that I didn't notice the man standing next to me.

"Hello sir, you must be Mr. D. We have been awaiting your arrival for a long time now."

Startled, I jumped and turned toward the voice.

A short Arabic man stood with his hands behind his back as if he was just waiting in a line. A big smile was plastered across his face. I was startled that he'd been able to sneak up on me so quietly, and with nothing around, I didn't even see him on our way in.

"Oh, yeah... Hi, I was just mesmerized by whatever … this ... uh...what is it?"

"These are what you people are here to help us understand. We will be starting immediately, once you have been settled. There is no time to waste."

The small assistant guided me to our tent. I pushed aside the entrance. The inside was pretty empty, only containing a few cots, desks, and footlockers for our equipment. I thanked the assistant and as I put my clothes away, I could hear the others still arguing as they approached. I did my best to just ignore them and focus on what I was to be researching. After a few minutes had passed, the assistant returned. He handed both Ms. T. and myself photos and samples of what the research team had recovered.

We spent the day reviewing those photos and coming up with several assumptions about the possible contents of the structure. However, what worried me most was that one of the walls appeared to have been a listing of the contents, almost as if it was some kind of manifest. The incredible creatures housed inside ranged from the mundane to things only seen in fantasy from what we could guess from the few pictures.

I called Ms. T. over to verify that my eyes weren't deceiving me. One of the pictographs showed the form of a human. Unknown symbols were present next to each engraving. We found dinosaurs in all manners of species, again with those strange symbols next to them.

"We have to get down there and see this up close," I said. "These photos aren't showing huge sections of these walls. We need to get inside."

Ms. T. agreed with me, and we notified the assistant. He seemed reserved on moving ahead of schedule however we didn't quite give him an option. Mr. J., although not thrilled, seemed quite intrigued at the notion of possibly getting a "fucking dino trophy," as he so elegantly put it.

The assistant notified someone over his phone of our decision before turning back to us and with a smile brought us to the opening of the shaft.

We had to wear special breathing equipment as well as all manners of climbing gear. We were informed that until the cave system was mapped fully, we should avoid it. However, there is a small team already down there who are about to open the structure. They radioed the team to wait until we could descend.

Almost as if on cue, the assistant's radio crackled and a voice said that they were able to find what appeared to be some sort of sliding door. When the team approached, it shot out a bright light before opening. They believed it to be some kind of scanner.

"A scanner? What kind of ancient civilization had access to biometrics?"

"Like the saucy tart from the plane said, the moppets are fucking aliens. Who knows what topsy-turvy shit is down there?"

The assistant responded letting them know that they should halt their incursion until we were able to meet up and join their expedition team. An annoyed voice said "affirmative," so we proceeded down into the dark seemingly-bottomless hole. It was much smaller than we thought it would be, maybe three to four feet wide at the most. Our equipment would scrape and bang off the walls as we were lowered into the depths.

I could hear Mr. J. attempting to speak, but over the noise of the wench and the echoing of the tunnel I couldn't understand a word he said. I thought to myself that it might be a blessing. Our descent took several minutes, and we finally emerged into an enormous cavern with work lights spread throughout the area, all pointing towards the monumental structure. The very sight of it left us all in awe.

Under the halogen lights, its surface was oily black, the walls intersecting edges were perfect ninety-degree angles, and the outside surface was covered with the same pictorial hieroglyphs. We were greeted by the team leader, who helped unhook us and got us up to speed with what they had discovered. They hadn't traveled inside yet, however, they'd discovered that almost every major earth event appeared to be depicted on the outside walls, with one major difference being made clear. All the depictions traced back to an engraving of the structure being placed here along with several others in a series of lines around an old Earth. Each new era of life, from Precambrian to modern man and further, to creatures that were beyond comprehension, appeared to be depicted on the surfaces.

However, there was something missing.

Ms. T. studied the pictographs closely, and after a few minutes she let out a gasp. "It's on a timer!"

What?

"Look here," she said, pointing at a place on the surface. "From the beginning when the monolith opened, it seeded the planet for certain evolutionary traits given the planet's ecosystem at the time. Whenever there was an unaccounted -for change, it is followed by a blank space where it would release the correct creatures to help mediate the planet's atmosphere and biosphere. Amazing! See here in this diagram, it shows one of these structures rising out of the earth somewhere near where we would call Rome, something is emanating from the top, drawing in the asteroid that killed off the dinosaurs, it doesn't have an empty spot and was immediately replaced by the smaller mammalian creatures that were able to survive the harsh ice age. Then here it shows the larger creatures being released such as the predator species to help bring balance. However down here these creatures have an empty space before a restart appears to have happened."

She bent over the images, a look of confusion on her face. "But something is still missing. Look here. It shows where modern homo sapiens are supposed to have gone extinct. Replaced by something else, but it looks like something happened because up here it shows them evolving to where we were two hundred years ago, but over there, those depictions end after where we currently are in our technological evolution. I believe this one here is our current timeline. However, there is a missing extinction level event meant to restart a new cycle... But since that didn't happen, the procedure halted."

"So we beat the system then, didn't we, what's the fucking problem?" Mr. J. said condescendingly.

"Well, *skitstovel*, perhaps you may remember what I said earlier about this thing seeming to release something to balance out the calculations for the ecosystem?"

"Yeah, what about it?"

I thought maybe I was getting it. "What she's saying is that since whatever was supposed to kill us off didn't happen, it's gone into a reset mode. Look at the pictures, it's blank because we weren't supposed to be here and find this. Something we do kills us and this thing is programmed to start the cycle over with something new. We need to get inside and find whatever might reset this and turn it off."

"Since when are you an expert on alien tech? It's a big black block a mile under the surface of a blazing sun. In the middle of a fucking desert."

"It doesn't take an expert to unplug something and needless to say, whatever comes out of that thing to balance everything isn't going to care where or what type of environment it is in. Plus, for all we know, this thing might cause some sort of nuclear winter or cause something to fall out of the sky like it did back to kill off the dinosaurs. If worse comes to worst we can at least see what it is planning and then we can try and come up with a counter to it."

"I don't know about you mate, but I got my countermeasures all sorted out right here with Mr. Boom-stick and I doubt anything is gonna keep coming after he starts talkin'."

Ms. T. and I looked at each other, both of us just astounded by the simple-minded thought process. We couldn't argue with such utter stupidity. With our responses so limited we had to walk away. Knowing what we had just discovered was something that changed this project from an amazing discovery to trying to uncover whether or not we are in fact trying to save the world as we know it.

We radioed base camp to notify them of Ms. T. 's theory and were told to wait for them to send down a few more armed men as security. There was no telling what may be inside of there.

We waited by the entry passage that the previous team had uncovered, and that's when I felt a feeling I had never felt before, a calming feeling mixed with a domineering aura. It was strange, looking down the smooth walled hallway. The unknown material that the structure was made from on the inside seemed to produce a light blue luminescence. Although the air around us felt damp, the general breeze coming from the interior hall felt dry and cool. I noticed a strange subtle smell, like there was a hint of mildew, but there was no visible source.

Ms. T. continued working to decipher any clues she could glean from the engravings, jotting down notes periodically, while Mr. J was throwing stones into the dark and listening to the echoes. We could see the armed men dropping down from the top of the cavern, their lights flickering as they spun slowly to the ground.

I wish I could remember their names. We had no idea what we were going to face down here and those men, the team, were only there because someone gave them an order. We all gathered by the entryway, a wave of emotions washing over us as we took those first steps into the truly unknown. The looks of amazement and fear were plastered over all their faces. The hall was completely empty, and something about the dry cool air just didn't seem right. The whole place seemed... wrong somehow.

No one spoke as we walked into the caverns. We were maybe a hundred yards in when one of the guards began to panic. Turning around, we saw what had spooked him. The door had, at some point, closed without a sound. That's when I realized what was wrong – there was no sound at all; it was as if someone hit the mute button on reality.

I watched as the others tried to scream, grabbing at their throats in disbelief. Mr. J. was trying to shout something, Ms. T. began frantically scribbling something in her notebook. One of the researchers ran back to the door. He beat his fists against the surface where the door once was, screaming to no avail, before turning back, walking as if having taken a major defeat.

I jumped as I felt a hand tap my shoulder. Turning around, I read the page forced in my face, black marker scribbled across it.

"WE NEED TO GO! WE MUST HAVE TRIGGERED SOME SORT OF TRAP!"

I nodded in agreement before tapping the others to get their attention. It took us a few minutes to regain our composure, but it was quite the adjustment.

We had the group gather as the guards took posts around us. The lead researcher stepped ahead of us in order to give direction. We had no other option at this point but to push forward. We eventually came to a wall that opened as they approached, revealing an all-black room, not dark, but as if made from obsidian on all sides. the same glowing light coming from everywhere and nowhere.

I felt another note being pushed into my hand.

"SHOULD WE GO IN?"

I pulled my pen out and scribbled before handing it back to Ms. T.

"DO WE HAVE A CHOICE?"

I stepped forward, thinking that it was crazy. *What is this?* Not knowing what to expect, I continued walking cautiously untilI hit the back wall. Feeling around, I turned back to give the all clear when I saw the others as if in slow motion, each in various degrees of stepping into the room. I waited long minutes, pacing through that room, checking the walls for any markings only to be met by their blackness.

Turning back, I watched as Mr. J. was the first to step foot into the room with me. As soon as his boot hit the floor his body sped up and his face said it all. He was scared.

He grabbed my shoulders and shook me trying to speak, only for his silence to be as realized in here as it was out there. In frustration he pushed back at me with annoyance.

We waited as, one by one, the others came through. Ms. T scribbled on her notepad again, handing me the note. I widened my eyes as I realized what it must have looked like from their perspective.

"WE JUMPED IN TO SAVE YOU, WE WERE SCARED SOMETHING HAPPENED. YOU WERE SUCKED INTO THE ROOM AND BEGAN RUNNING AROUND AS IF ON FAST FORWARD."

I wrote back, *"It was the exact opposite from here. You all were moving in slow motion and I didn't know if I should go back."*

The room grew dark as the door we passed through closed. Flashlights turned on and their light splashed our faces. I felt my stomach lurch as if I was on a roller coaster before it suddenly stopped. A bright light flooded the room as the doors opened again.

Mr. J., Ms. T. and I all stepped out at the same time. Soon followed by the others. It seemed as if the room's strange effects were only for where we were. We found ourselves in a new hallway, but this one was different from the others we'd been in. Tubes lined the walls, vertically stacked in a staggered pattern up to the ceiling. The screens were next to each one like monitors of some sort, tucked into the open spaces as if placed for filling in the empty air rather than efficiency. I walked over and saw that they displayed more of those pictoglyphs. They appeared to show what was originally housed in them. A large empty sack made from some sort of clear plastic was above each container. It was like something out of a sci-fi movie.

Judging by the pictures it looked like it was some form of primate or neanderthal. I touched the screen and a long line of various depictions of animals was displayed. The first symbol being that of the outside of the structure, open with a depiction of it closed at the end. I couldn't believe it still worked. These must have been some sort of stasis tubes or something. This... this was a phenomenal find. The mass of knowledge we could gather from these alone would revolutionize everything.

I felt a tap on my shoulder again as one of the researchers alerted me that the group was moving ahead. I had to tear myself away from the screen, but made a mental note that when we returned to the surface that this needed to be researched heavily.

Walking in total silence was very unnerving in these new surroundings, but knowing that there was a chance something alive was released in here at some point added a new layer to my anxiety. Every one of the researchers looked on in wonder at the presence of a still-operational stasis chamber. I know that I felt like a kid in a candy castle, stopping periodically to look at whatever must have been held in them at some point in an ancient time. Although we couldn't yet read what was written, it would only be a matter of time before we would know the secrets.

We eventually arrived at a ramp leading down into a very large space reminiscent of a warehouse. All sizes of stasis chambers were open and lined the room. Some were big enough to hold full sized adult elephants if not larger.

We couldn't believe what we were looking at. This whole facility was like some huge ark or a… lab.

Walking through the massive room, I stopped periodically and clicked random buttons on the various screens to see if anything would happen. Occasionally the doors would close and different colored lights would flash before a red symbol appeared on the screen.

It took longer than we thought it would to simply cross the room, seeing as there seemed to be a broken or shattered glass-like substance that one of the guards found out the hard way. It sliced through the leather and rubber sole of his boot as if it was tissue paper, causing a deep cut on the bottom of his foot.

After fixing the wound we had to traverse the obstacles it presented, and it made us have to find alternate routes across the room.. It was like a razor blade-studded minefield in some areas, almost as if it had been purposefully placed. The last thing we needed was some kind of ancient infection setting in.

As remarkable as all this was, we had to remember that this was unknown territory for every field and at any point the wrong button could spell disaster.

We managed to make it to the other side of this room that somehow seemed larger than what the outside of the building would allow. There, we came across a massive doorway.

The door appeared to have taken some damage, but was still closed. Once again, a bright light scanned us before the door began to rise. If sound wasn't absorbed in here, it probably would have deafened us as the metallic stone-looking parts folded up into the frame. like some kind of reverse tetris. Each section fit perfectly into its place and the door was gone.

Another large room greeted us, however this time the stasis tubes had not all been opened. We entered cautiously and discovered that the tubes held for the most part what appeared to be relatively normal-looking animals. Granted, they were less evolved than our surface animals; however, all the creatures appeared to be dehydrated. Large sacks were suspended above the stasis tubes and each one was filled with a dark reddish liquid.

Incredibly, there were creatures thought to have become extinct or have been extinct for centuries in some of the tubes. Inspection of the open tubes and cells showed that they had at one point contained species we recently have seen making recoveries in small numbers in hidden colonies. We'd had no idea how they had stayed hidden for so long however this seemed to show that they had possibly been released.

The excitement that I was experiencing was killing me. I knew we were here to see what was going to end us; however, these discoveries were just overwhelming to say the least. Looking around, I saw the other researchers as well as our security personnel looking in wonder as the dehydrated creatures were curled up. How had they gotten here? Who was collecting them? Were they grown?

I felt Ms. T. place her hand on my shoulder again, her face had a confused look. The paper she held had the best question that hadn't occurred to me in all this wonderment.

"How would any of these things cause our extinction?"

She was right, none of these things contained anything that could cause an extinction, or indeed, anything out of the ordinary. If this is what we could see, then what were we missing?

One of the researchers rushed over from one of the terminals. He grabbed my arm practically dragging me over to where he had been typing. He had somehow pulled up what looked like a schematic of the facility. From what we could see according to the screen, this complex had at least another several miles of floors beneath our current position, each with different dimensions expanding far beyond what the external part we could see topside. Several of which had tunnels of some sort or outlets leading to nearby bodies of saltwater and freshwater areas. The map also showed another structure adjacent to the building we were in, although much smaller in comparison and only containing three sub-floors. It appeared to be located not too far into the cave system. We tried selecting the building only to be met with a symbol we guessed indicated 'Access Denied.'

The researcher motioned for a piece of paper and began to write.

"We need to get out of here, from what I can see this is just a warehouse. The control area must be this building."

We could see that the way we came in wasn't the only way out. There appeared to be another exit from a floor just below where we were now. Some sort of a ramp led up to a lift. Clicking on the floor plan showed an icon none of us had seen on the screen before. It looked like a tablet with writing, almost like a library icon. It was a small room in comparison to the others on screen. Maybe it was some sort of records room. One could only imagine what kind of information was stored there.

With the path ahead of us appearing to be pretty straightforward, we gathered the others and headed back to the elevator. As much as I wanted to stay and investigate everything, the silence was becoming incredibly disorientating. The researcher and Ms. T. were able to figure out the sequence for the elevator to take us back up. This floor must have been a predetermined destination for whoever built this place. They must have come here frequently, because it was surprisingly easy to select a floor from the terminal. We all looked at each other, a little nervous about entering the lift again, but in the end, we all boarded. The trip only took a few seconds, and we felt a collective trepidation as the doors opened. What we saw confirmed our concern: The floor was littered with both mummified and decomposed corpses; some looked almost human yet they were almost ten feet tall. Their heads and exposed skulls were also elongated with matted hair attached where skin still clung.

"What the fuck!"

We all turned to look at Mr. J., surprised to hear anything. In our shock, we hadn't noticed that whatever had caused the silence wasn't active here.

"Shh." Ms. T. raised her hand to her mouth.

"What are you goin' on about? They are clearly dead."

"Yes, you idiot, but whatever killed them might still be here."

"Lady, look at those dried out pricks, whatever got them must have died off long ago."

"We don't know that!"

"Fuck lady, we just spent the last few hours in complete quiet. Let me enjoy some noise."

As those two argued, one of the armed men stepped into the room. Each step reverberated in my head as my ears adjusted. He stopped panning his flashlight over something and waved us over to check it out. His confusion was obvious on his face.

We carefully stepped over the remains, making our way closer to the man. His look became more understandable as we saw what he was seeing. The creature laying at his feet was far different from the bodies surrounding it.

The creature was like nothing we saw on that lower floor. It was massive; if it were to stand up in the room it wouldn't shock me if its head was touching the ceiling. From what we could tell, it was face down and the skin of its right arm looked to be peeled back, revealing an opening containing thousands of thin needle-like teeth, each the size of my pinky. Its skin was translucent, as if all the moisture had been drained.

One of the guards seemed curious as we studied the creature. He grabbed the oddly bent arm and lifted the mouth open. The sound of the dried skin stretching and cracking under the stress was like peeling dried sinew off a dog bone.

"Hey, what are you doing? Don't touch it!" I said.

I don't know if he didn't understand what I was saying or just ignoring me, but the look on his face said I needed to see what was inside.

Stepping over the creature's head, I looked down and saw one of the other humanoids was wrapped inside. Its body was covered in thousands of tiny holes as if it was encased in some kind of biological iron maiden. But why? What purpose was there to this creature's existence? Scanning over what I could see, I was surprised to see several small sacks still filled with some kind of viscous fluid that looked like small water balloons.

"Ow! Fuckers are still sharp."

I was so lost in my thoughts that I hadn't noticed the guard trying to pull out one of the teeth. The cut he had inflicted upon himself was coating the tooth with his blood.

A shudder ran through me. "Get your hand away from it. Who knows what diseases or viruses this thing is carrying. You gotta be more..."

Before I could finish chastising the guard, a licking sound drew all of our attention. One of the sacks drained down and the creature's tongue started to slowly engorge as it re-hydrated. We stared in paralyzing horror as it began to lick the fresh blood off its loosened tooth.

I looked back at the sacks and a cold chill ran up my spine as they began to pulsate spreading its contents into the surrounding membranes. Its skin began to flush out with streaks as the thick blood-like substance spread.

"Oi mate? Maybe we should... you know make like a tree and get the fuck out of here huh?" The worry in Mr.

J.'s voice was enough for me to understand that even he knew when it was time to go.

Ms. T. and I looked at each other and back to Mr. J in a panic-filled motion of agreement. We began stepping back slowly from the creature's body, which was now swelling as it re-hydrated to more than twice the size it had been only a few minutes ago. Its mouth closed on the arm and hand clenching it.

The bleeding guard took a few steps back before the creature's monstrous arm shot out and grabbed his leg. It unwrapped its mouth and slammed him against the ceiling as it began to rise to its full height. The soldier struggled in the vice-like grip before his flailing body was slammed down to the ground with a bone-shattering crunch.

The previously mummified husk dropped from its now engorged residence before the monster wrapped its maw over and around the screaming man. For a moment, its body contracted and shivered before it unfurled itself, dropping the drained remains of the man to the floor.

I was in so much shock that I hadn't even heard the gunshots as the other guards opened fire, their bullets tearing through the monster's soft flesh. Mr. J. grabbed my arm, pulling me away from the creature. I saw that he was also dragging Ms. T. away.

"Snap out of it mate! We gotta go!"

He dragged us behind a strange computer as the others scattered. The towering monster was relentless as it grabbed another security team member, ripping his arm off, the rifle still firing as it dropped to the floor. The creature repeated its ingestion of the guard, just as it had its previous victim. Dropping his slime-covered body to the floor after draining their fluids. A large protruding sack seemed to be filled on the monster's back now.

I looked over my shoulder to the others. Ms. T. was just staring straight ahead, still in shock. Mr. J. fumbled with the gun case he had slung on his shoulder. From behind us, the gunshots went silent as another muffled scream was snuffed out, followed by another squishing sound. I closed my eyes, hoping I would wake up from this nightmare. The pure mental stress of everything since stepping out my door yesterday pushed me to the border of insanity.

"Oi buddy! You still with me"

I opened my eyes. Mr. J. had his hand on my shoulder. His other arm hefting what looked to me to be a gigantic shotgun.

"Now listen. I need you to do me a favor."

I looked at him not knowing what to say.

"Okay good, now I'm gonna head over here with Mr. Boom-stick, I need you to get that big gits attention and get him to come over here and say 'ello. Alright? And go!"

Before I could even respond to the absolutely batshit crazy idea, he was off. I looked to Ms. T. for some clarification, but she was still catatonic. I really didn't want anything to do with this plan.

Hesitantly, I peered out from behind my cover just in time to see the monster grab another researcher as it stalked through the aisles of strange computer-like stones. The flailing man had some sort of a spiked hammer, and he began hitting the creature's hand repeatedly before it quickly whipped him to the floor. I watched him try to rise, broken bones visibly jutting out of his body. The creature reached down, picked the broken man up before muffling him with its embrace.

I was hyperventilating as I heard a sharp whistle. I turned to see Mr. J. was in place and was signaling me to act. I took a deep breath. But before I could do anything, Ms. T. sprinted forward, screaming like a banshee. I spun my head as thunderous footsteps and a mass of crushing bone came rushing our way. I rose to get its attention in time to hear a deafening explosion and the creature's side blew out, staggering it to a knee. A second shot rang out as its giant cycloptic eye in the center of its head burst like a giant water balloon. The heavy lump falling forward, all the blood it had drained from the others now rushing out of it in a river, pooling at my feet.

My ears rang and my body wobbled, regaining its equilibrium as a worried looking Mr. J. walked over to me. He was trying to ask me something, but all I could hear was a muffled voice mixed with a high-pitched hum. Pointing to my ears, he took his hands off my shoulders and walked behind me while laughing and patting me on the back. This must not have been his first near death experience with a violent animal.

Ms. T. was huddled in the fetal position rocking back and forth behind one of the stone computer towers. Mr. J. crouched down beside her, wrapped his arm around her. She had been so strong up until this point, but now she looked like a scared child gripping her father's jacket. I can't say I blamed her.

Looking back at the creature its body began to shrink down and dry out as all the fluids drained from the massive wounds. My hearing returned as some of the other researchers came out of their hiding spots. There were only five of us now, the three of us, the computer engineer and the leader who had greeted us when we first got down here.

The leader said something to the computer guy and he began typing on a nearby monitor. Mr. J. came walking over with Ms. T. under his arm. She was looking down at the floor and mumbling something to herself.

"Oi mate, we gotta get out of here. She's not doin' too good."

"Y-yeah, let's... let's ask them, maybe they've figured out how to get out of here."

We sidestepped around the almost re-mummified creature towards the other survivors and before we could say anything, a bright light illuminated the area, and a voice in a language none of us could understand. Its tone echoed throughout the chamber. I looked at Mr. J. as the light changed to a bluish-white hue and the walled door slid open.

The rush of the hot humid air was welcomed at this point. We didn't want to hesitate and get stuck inside, so we all rushed out, collapsing to the hard stone floor once we were clear. It took a second for me to open my eyes as I thanked whatever was out there for letting me survive what we just went through. My thoughts were interrupted by the realization that the floor of the cave was lit up.

Looking up there was now a large dug out hole where we had come in. Huge cables ascended up towards the light and an elevator of sorts rested on a landing. We could hear voices echoing from the cave that we were told to avoid.

We had the researchers take Ms. T. to the lift. Mr. J. and I walked over to the cave entrance. We hadn't even made it halfway before hearing screams and gunfire erupting from the shadowed hallway. A loud crash of metal reverberated as a large mangled piece of tank tread came flying through the entrance.

Several people dressed in military clothes came rushing out of the hole, shooting at whatever was coming. A familiar-looking man in a blood-stained shirt was mixed in among them. The earth rattled as whatever it was got closer. The soldiers ran past us like we weren't even there as a massive clawed hand with a toothy mouth in its palm reached through the archway, grabbing one of the poor men and pulling him back. His screams were cut short by tearing clothes and flesh. Whatever had grabbed him was much larger than what we'd faced in the computer room.

Fortunately, it was simply too large to fit through the entryway. Several loud thuds followed by boulders, crashed against the walls as it tried breaking through.

I ran over to the familiar man who was now bent over the railing of some kind of walkway near a cavern. His head in the crook of his arm gasping for breath in his mask.

"What the hell was that thing"

His head shot up and a look of surprise and confusion matching mine as I realized that the man I was looking at was the same man that had sent us down here only a few hours ago, yet he was so much older.

"How... How is... Is that really you?" He stammered.

"What happened? What was that thing?"

He flinched as another boulder smashed the wall.

"We thought you were all dead."

"What do you mean? We've only been in there a few hours?"

"Hours? Sir, it has been ten years."

"Ten years? There is no way.... That... Oh god, the elevator." It took me a minute to understand the situation, but it slowly sank in.

Another crash echoed when the look on the assistant's face dropped. It sounded like glass shattering.

"Everyone to the lift! Now!"

More sounds of broken glass filled the room from the cavern as we ran for the elevator. If whatever was coming was anything like what we saw in that room, then multiples of them would be hell.

I turned to see several gray figures. There were two of the large monsters from before with maybe ten or so smaller creatures crawling across the ground on all fours like dogs mixed with gorillas. The larger ones began to run, closing the gap with each of their strides.

One of the soldiers hit the 'Up' button and pulled a lever as we ran, my heart racing. The thought of being stuck down here with those things terrified me.

I could hear the galloping-like pounding as the smaller ones neared. Another scream came from behind us, followed by it being muffled before a squishy crunch snuffed it out completely. I turned to see one of the smaller creatures had engulfed his head and was now past his shoulders. With each undulation, it twitched as if biting down, crushing the body, swallowing him whole. Red sacks filled up like tumors bulging from its stretching skin. Another man fell and was dragged into the creature's smooth anus-like mouth. He struggled to free himself, only to be overpowered. It grabbed at his body, forcing him to bend and twist as it forced him down its throat, each contraction forcing blood and entrails out of his mouth like a hellish tube of toothpaste.

I panicked as I saw the lift begin to rise. I sprinted and was able to get a hand on the ledge of the platform. I felt someone grab my arm and another grab my shirt, lifting me up to the platform. My body slumped onto the metal grating as gunfire erupted. Mr. J grabbed his gun and the concussive blasts tore through the air as one of the small creatures blew almost completely in half. As the hole closed in around us, I finally felt some semblance of safety. Very few had made it out but I noticed that the man I thought of as 'the assistant' had also managed to get on in time.

Below us we heard the sound of a wall collapsing down followed by thuds of footsteps dying off in the distance as we ascended.

Walking over I grabbed the assistant by the shoulders and shook him, asking what the hell they had done. He turned to me and he looked remorseful.

"I don't know how it happened. We were just trying to bring out a few of the creatures for research purposes. We thought they were dead."

"What are you talking about? I want to know how ten years have passed and no one tried to help us!"

"We did! We tried to get in where your team entered, but it was just a wall by the time we got there. We tried everything including explosives and hardened drills. Nothing penetrated whatever that thing is made out of, not even a scratch. After a month, we assumed your team was lost. There just wasn't any way that you had enough food or water to survive. In the meantime, we had discovered the other construct."

"Yeah, we saw that on a computer in the building. A lot of symbols that looked like warning signs came up when we tried to access it to look at what it had inside.

The assistant snorted. "Oh, we found out alright. We found that the first few floors were nothing but storage tubes with various creatures suspended in them."

"Were they all dried out like mummies?"

"No. Well not yet. Let me explain.

"We approached and much like what your team experienced, a bright light seemed to scan us and we went into the building. After that we took an elevator to a lower level filled with thousands of stasis tubes looking like something out of some mad scientist's wet dream. Those creatures were all suspended in what looked like vacuum sealed bags and dried out like you said, almost completely mummified yet from the monitors they showed what looked like life signs. It took years for us to catalog what we could. We eventually discovered what looked like a clock. The symbols we determined to be going in a strange pattern until someone made a comment that they repeated in intervals."

"A timer?"

"Think of it as an alarm clock. One of the engineers figured out how to speed it up so that we could open one of the tubes. When we did, we saw this blood sack suspended above it constricted like a muscle and it forced its contents into the creature. We tried to stop it but ended up freeing several others. Those smaller creatures wiped out almost our whole team before we were able to take them down. It was another costly mistake and since then, we have taken all precautions far more seriously."

"But what was that big creature? How did that get free?"

"The timer hit zero. See, when we were inside, we found the control room. We found a body of a creature over one of the terminals. Turns out that we weren't the only species to have evolved on this planet, or found this place. Whoever they were, they managed to decipher the language of the builders and changed the timer, extending it, and in doing so released several types of hominids... Our ancestors."

"How is that possible? According to the other buildings' hieroglyphs it's a cycle where life ends and begins again. All the glyphs showed that we were only supposed to make it to certain points of evolution, then it goes to a grayed-out area."

"Yes, we saw that too, but we also found that each extinction event seemed to happen at almost exact time intervals, as if after each major event the world was wiped clean and restarted, being allowed to evolve a little further before again being erased. It was as if it was some weird science experiment testing different eras of civilization against whatever would eventually erase them."

"Why were you taking them out of here though if they were already secured. Why not just lock the place down?

"We didn't have time, once we understood what we had discovered. We found the files and from what we could understand there is no stopping this countdown, only postponing it."

"Can't we just postpone it again like the ones before us?"

"Unfortunately, we can't. We tried everything and our only option would be to initiate final countdown procedures to restart the system and put in a new release date. Whoever our predecessors were, they tried to give us a chance. The times they entered seem to stagger when these creatures are released. As far as we can tell this was to keep things manageable."

"Manageable? What are you talking about?"

"The people that came before us were survivors of their extinction event. I don't know how they did it, but they had a way.

They have been referenced throughout time and in most religions. However, we have kept their interactions labeled as visions or angels. Stories were written which made them out as deities. They brought us knowledge and skills. They trained us to farm and fight like soldiers.

The people we work for are from a long family line going back thousands of years who were originally entrusted with keeping these secrets."

"However, our job now, since discovering this as well as other locations, is to catalog and extract which creatures are close to revival and hopefully kill them. The organization that employs us has been around for millennia. Searching for these facilities with no luck until a decade ago when we happened across this one and the plan was finally implemented for destroying them.

The few that escaped over the centuries have become legends and folklore. The Greeks and Romans called them Titans, old English stories tell of dragons,

Norwegians called them trolls. Our organization has hunted them down and killed as many as possible but we are running out of time. We had no clue the true scale of the situation. Our predecessors never gave us the locations only the warning to stay away"

The ground around us began to quake. As harsh as it was, it stopped suddenly. The silence was only interrupted by the humming of the lift's motors. A few seconds later it was as if World War three had started above us. Gunfire could be heard followed by explosions. I looked at the scared little man only to see him crying.

"We're too late."

We broke the surface into a war zone. Men were behind cover shooting at an absolutely massive creature. It reached down grabbing soldiers feeding them into a mass of arms and hands where the creature's face should be, before being torn to pieces and devoured by tiny mouths on the palms of each hand. Its humanoid body was built like an athlete, but it was fifty or more feet tall. A giant stasis tube was protruding out of a crack in the desert. We felt the earth tremble again as more of the large tubes began to emerge.

Jets began launching missiles and firing on the unopened containers, destroying those they could before re-hydration could be completed. We all scattered from the platform. The soldiers that were with us opened fire. Mr. J., Ms. T., the assistant and I all ran for cover, watching as our world appeared to crumble all around us. Several smaller tubes began to push their way through the sand releasing the smaller smooth skinned creatures.

We ran towards an SUV only to be cut off by a series of tubes raising out of the earth and then hissing open. Mr. J opened fire on the glass tubes, the heavy rounds blowing through whatever they were made of and painting the insides with thick black and red slop.

We all crammed into the vehicle, only to find it didn't have the key in it. We felt the car lift up slightly into the air as fingers dug into the roof before ripping it off, dropping it back to the ground. A mass of arms wriggled and contorted as they grasped towards us. One of the mouthed hands grabbed Ms. T,'s arm wrenching her out of the seat with a sickening pop as her body seemed to fall limp from her shoulder. We grabbed her wherever we could reach and held on. I looked up to see all the piranha-like mouths ripping and tearing the flesh from the bone of her arm. The ease at which they broke human bones was frightening.

We managed to free her from the creature's grip when Mr. J. blasted it with both barrels point blank, sending it staggering back blood rushing from the wounds. Seconds later its body was torn apart from machine gun fire by a passing jet.

Before we could run again, a small squad came to us and got us to an awaiting helicopter. As we rose up out of the danger zone we watched as tanks rolled in.

We were taken to a nearby military base where they immediately separated us. We were interrogated and debriefed about what had happened and how we managed to survive a decade without aging. It was just such a surreal experience. We were all informed that we didn't have a choice anymore. We either had to accept the situation and continue working for them or spend the rest of our lives in an asylum. I was scared, but accepted the offer. I haven't seen the others since, but through the grapevine I heard Ms. T. was treated for her injuries and has been hospitalized since she never came out of her shock. Mr. J. chose to become a guard; however, he vanished along with one of the captured small creatures.

We later found out It took several hours before the larger beasts were finally brought down and days to clean up the straggling smaller creatures that managed to get to local population centers.

In all we lost almost a hundred units that day, and two small towns were bombed. It was a major adjustment afterwards because we weren't allowed to talk about what we had seen or experienced. The whole thing was brushed under the rug by explaining it away as an assault on an underground terrorist cell. It was scary how easily they were able to spin a story and the fight in the desert was nothing more than just another firefight.

That was the day that my responsibilities began with this organization and what has led me to our current predicament.

I plan on going through as many files as I can and dictating those of interest that might pose a significant threat in the future for whoever listens to them.

Recording File-005 - Code Name "UNDER THE MOUNTAIN"

(*T-minus three hours before impact.*)

"The next series of recordings are going to be a little out of order, sorry about that. However, given that the timer has been reset and now we only have a few more hours due to the chunk of shell that is hurtling toward us faster since that thing used it as a push off point... the accelerated speed has cut our time together forcing me to move locations and I dropped the file folders. figures I'd fuck up now huh? Anyways, I think I'm going to have to skim the details with these next few files and give a more... Cliff-Notes version. So I think it's time for another sip, and here we go."

I searched through the old folders, finally landing on this one. I said into my microphone, "Oh here's a good one."

~

We had picked up the survivors just outside of Bhutan. They were attempting to climb a mountain in the area that for "spiritual" reasons was made illegal to climb. There had been several rumors of strange creatures inhabiting the caves in the area. However, that did not persuade our trespassers there away from the area, and now two of their group were confirmed dead and one is still missing to this day, but assumed dead.

I was heading down to interrogation to find out what they were doing there and how they managed to survive. The two individuals had been given cover names and had also been kept separated at the time so that we were able to get more information.

This wasn't too long after my first few missions, so I was starting to get the groove of what my new position was, as well as just how much I could get away with, but I digress.

When we picked them up, the male – from here on out he will be designated as "Smalls" in the file – was half beaten to death. He had sustained several significant injuries consistent with those found in people who have fallen from great heights, but he seemed terrified of the extremely tall woman who we had found standing over his broken body. So we made a judgment call.

His jaw was broken in three places so our hopes of a verbal conversation were dashed. However, he was still able to type with one hand. We provided a laptop and he was currently writing out his experience. I was going in to debrief the other survivor.

The woman – we have designated her as "Bigs" in the file – appears physically fine, other than a few bumps and bruises. She was still in shock and hadn't said too much other than "they were so big."

We moved her to isolation given that the context we found them in was questionable at best. It appeared that she had attacked Smalls and given her clear size, she'd dominated him.

I think what I'm going to do from here on out is attach the files to each recording, so please see the accompanying paperwork for the actual file designation as well as the brief reports and any recordings that are associated with them.

Incident report

File Name: <u>Under the mountain</u>

Precautions to be taken:

Area to be quarantined and a cover story of hazardous climbing and avalanche warnings to be put in place.

- Armed patrols are to be carried out around the perimeter every hour.

- No personnel are allowed access without director's specific instruction.

- All creatures found to have escaped are to be captured or neutralized.

All files from here on out have been edited to keep the identities of those involved safe and controlled.

Case # 005

Subject 1: "Bigs"

Location found: along a service road just outside of the quarantine zone.

Description: 6'2" Female, roughly 170 lbs, large athletic build, brunette, brown eyes, aggressive temperament.

Subject 2: "Smalls"

Location found: Service Road, same location as Subject 1.

Description: 5'4" Caucasian male, approximately 140 lbs, blue eyes, thin athletic build, short blond hair.

~

Upon entering the small interrogation room, I noticed that the subject was very calm and collected. She had been in isolation for several days before she was able to properly communicate due to when we were able to zero in on their location. It was a questionable circumstance and we believe at the time her irrational behavior was based upon her experience in the structure.

Carrying a stack of pictures recovered from a camera that was retrieved on site, I had several questions to ask her about their little excursion. As it turns out, these two survivors managed to not only survive climbing up as high as they did, but also managed to get out of the mountain in a very unusual location. meaning that our initial measurements were way off.

"Hello Ms. Bigs, how are you doing today?"

I tried to muster my best bedside manners, but I already knew her game. Even if she wasn't responsible for her friend's injuries I personally didn't wanna get into a physical altercation with her.

She shifted a bit and her visual confusion and fear was now more evident knowing that where she was didn't appear to be someplace she wanted to be stuck. "Given the circumstances, how do you think I'm doing?"

"Well, it's good to see your experience hasn't ruined your ability to be sarcastic, but please I am only here to help and I assure you that once our investigation is completed and you have been thoroughly debriefed, you will be free to go."

"The hell does that mean? I'm being debriefed, about what? The giant freaking monsters that ate or ripped my group apart? What else is there to tell you? We just wanted to hike and climb someplace new and unexplored. How were we supposed to know that that place existed and those beasts of horror were there?"

I was caught off guard by her very aggressive nature, I mean I was warned by the other agent she had a bit of an entitled attitude, but again I wrote it off as just stress, especially given that I wasn't the one to usually do the interviews.

"I understand that you are upset, ma'am, however, this is a necessary step in determining the threat level you and your knowledge pose to the secrecy of that facility."

"The threat I pose? How about you answer some of my questions and maybe then I will answer yours!"

"If I had the information to give you, I would, especially if it meant speeding this up, but the case at hand is we weren't even aware of this particular construct until we found you and your partner there."

I knew we had been lying to her, but I don't think she knew that we had been monitoring that mountain for a long time. It was in a strange area where we had found several escaped human-sized specimens.

"So you know about these things?" She said cutting me off.

I looked at the mirror for confirmation as to what I was allowed to discuss. I received a message stating that I was allowed to divulge the information given that she was already aware of the location.

"Yes ma'am, there are actually quite a few, and there are more popping up each day. Our goal here is to find them and keep them from opening or releasing the creatures contained within the structure. That would cause an extinction level event so massive that it would end all life on earth as we know it. So if you please, may we continue?"

The woman's demeanor changed now that the gravity of the situation was settling in. "What happens if one of these locations becomes active?"

"We don't know yet, however, we have had agents that survived the first encounter say that just a few of the larger creatures took out several tanks before being brought down by mobile artillery. I don't know what lies within each facility, but they appear to be location-based and designed for those particular environments."

Rubbing her eyes, she seemed to be in quite a bit of distress. "I need a few minutes please. This... this is just a lot to take in all at once."

"I understand, but please keep in mind there is a time limit and the faster we get the intel from you on how things happened, the faster we can shut down this facility and keep it neutralized."

She nodded her understanding and I gave her some time to acclimate to the reality of the situation.

As I left the room a voice chirped in my earpiece.

"You know she's hiding something, right?"

"I'm aware, however, until we know what she did in there, and why she beat the hell out of the other guy, we can't really move too fast or far. Besides, our teams are still excavating the site so we can gain access through the way they exited."

"I understand that you are also aware of the fact that all these locations have a timer – three of which have already counted down and are currently contained, but not yet neutralized."

"Yes sir, but I do not want to jump straight to more drastic interrogation if it is not needed."

There was a short pause followed by a sigh. "You have one day to get her to talk or get something out of ShortStack in there that we can use."

"Understood." With that I turned off my radio to head back into the small room, where the woman was now sobbing.

"Ma'am, it's okay, you are not in any trouble, but I do need to know what happened."

She took several deep breaths and seemed to start to calm down after a few minutes. "We just wanted to hike a trail and climb the mountain no one else had climbed before."

"We know, you have already told us that part several times, but we need to know what happened, where you entered the cave, everything you can remember so that my teams can do what they have to do in order to keep the rest of humanity safe. Yet for some reason, after all this time, you seem to be avoiding the whole situation in the middle as far as anything past the very beginning and the very end."

Again, she started to whimper, but quickly collected herself. "We started on the south side of the mountain, there is a small goat trail and the group we were with were all experienced mountain climbers. We had all met each other at another smaller mountain that we all seemed to frequent."

"Garry was a doctor who would go there to relax, but seemed bored having done the same place so many times."

"Samantha, but we just called her Sam, was a relative newbie, but was very capable when it came to gathering resources and could fit into most tight areas to set equipment or ropes and hook ups."

"Then there was "Smalls" and his girlfriend. both very experienced climbers. They said they worked in the tech industry."

Taking my notes, it sounded like quite the little landing party. "And what about yourself?"

"I was the unofficial organizer of the expedition. More or less a trail tracker and guide, planner if you will."

"So you all just happened to meet up and decided to climb one of the most dangerous mountains on Earth? And an illegal mountain to climb, I might add."

"I never said we were the brightest group of people." She said with a tinge of attitude.

"Ma'am there is no need to be short with me. Please continue."

"Fine. We were doing great on time and were where we needed to be, but after a slight issue on the goat trail we'd planned to take – it was impassable due to rock slides – we managed to clear a path and continue on our way via an alternate route."

"You cleared it how?"

"One of the guys had a collapsible shovel on his pack, the rest of us used what we could in order to help."

"It couldn't have been much, was it?"

"No, it only took the five of us maybe a few minutes before we managed to dig enough of the bottom out that the remainder slid down the side. Basically, it cleared itself."

She shifted a bit more in her seat and became more relaxed as she spoke, like a weight was being lifted from her.

"So we managed to make it about another mile up this mountain before "Smalls" spotted a large opening into the side of a cliff face, maybe forty feet up off the trail. The strange bit was that there was a thick rope that dangled out from it about twenty feet from the entrance. He and his girlfriend wandered up ahead of us to see if there was a way up to it and then they excitedly waved us over. We all stood there as he explained that we should check it out and maybe there might be some cool stuff in there. He made it sound like it wouldn't take too much time out of our trek and that maybe there would be clues to a better way up."

"I decided to search ahead to be sure our path was clear and found that unfortunately where we had just dug out wasn't the only place where a rock slide had blocked the path. So I made my way back to the group who had already begun climbing and setting anchor points. Smalls' girlfriend was already at the top putting the final anchor in place when I told them the bad news."

"They were obviously a little annoyed seeing as it is not cheap to fly to where we were – not to mention the difficulty of finding someone willing to take us as far as they did due to superstition and religious beliefs."

I laughed a bit at her comment because we ran into another facility hidden behind what was known as the "Final door" that was located in India. They believed that it held an untold amount of wealth, but from what a deeply embedded agent was able to gather, the door was built with the other sections sealed as a way to keep the creatures it held within from escaping. The treasures that were left in each "Vault" were meant to keep would-be prying eyes away, and the final vault held the entryway into that particular facility. The vault doors have since been resealed and the final door has also been permanently sealed after the exploratory team managed to gain access to the main computer bank room and disable the release timer, which we had inadvertently set off when we entered the building.

Bigs continued her story. She talked about how after they all managed to get inside the cave, they decided to explore, seeing as their main route had been completely blocked. They wanted to see if maybe one of the tunnels would open up to the other side of the blockage, but instead one of their group almost fell into a massive open area that seemed to descend for miles. The mountain seemed to be completely hollow, except for the gigantic cube-like structure suspended and eight massive chains affixed one to each corner, stone pathways leading up to it.

"We were in complete awe when we saw the object. Honestly, we thought we were having a collective hallucination, like we were possibly breathing in some kind of toxic gas and we were just tripping before we'd eventually died. I mean, knowing what I know now... I kind of wish that that had been the case. I wish we had just turned around and left."

"So whose idea was it to go inside?"

"That would be Mr. Smart Ass himself, 'Smalls'.

I was beginning to see a pattern here and I wasn't sure that this was the truth. *Somehow this scrawny rock climber managed to commandeer an entire mountaineering expedition in the span of a few hours?* Looking at this beast of a woman, I had serious doubts that her story was believable, but I had to give the powers that be *something*.

She continued on about the climbs they had to do to eventually get to one of the many doorways, and much like when I had my experience, they too were scanned. With some trepidation, according to Ms. Biggs, they entered the ark.

"Ms. Bigs, would you mind telling me just for the record – what was the date that you entered the facility?"

Confused, she began thinking of what the date was and it dawned on me. She's not aware of what year or day it is.

"It was June 6, 2006, why?"

"Has anyone told you what today is?"

"No, I've been kept in this room and in a cell for the last few days. Why?"

Taking my glasses off I rubbed my eyes for the inevitable freak out that was about to occur.

"Ma'am... it is October 25, 2021... you've been missing for fifteen years."

Her mouth dropped and she began to hyperventilate. "What? How? it couldn't have been more than maybe eight hours. We were only out for maybe a day."

This wasn't the first time someone had a panic attack finding out they've been gone over a decade. Hell, I remember when the realization hit *m*e on our way back from the battlefield to the main base. I'd been sitting in the very chair this woman was now crying in as I was debriefed on what we saw and went through. Not gonna lie, at this point I'm not surprised when people lose their shit. However, 'Century Man' from the last place we found was beyond helpful. His knowledge of the facilities laid the groundwork on how we shut them down now. When we found him, he was huddled in a corner of some city mumbling to himself, because the last thing he remembered before his adventure was that he once saw wooden ships floating by the island he lived on, before his people eventually became the aboriginals in Australia. This was about fifty thousand years ago, which from our calculations he experienced as just under three of our years while inside the cube; 2.68 years, to be exact.

This woman had no idea how bad her situation would have been had they not found an exit.

"It's okay ma'am, when you are ready, we can continue."

It took a little longer than the others, but she did eventually relax again, at least enough to continue.

"Where am I going to go? Will my family remember me? What would I even tell them?" she asked, rapid fire.

"We have already begun writing up a plausible story for where you have been."

"What's the story?"

"That isn't important right now."

"What do you mean 'It isn't important'?

"Fate of the world, ma'am, please continue and I promise you everything will be okay."

She sat there, a look of disbelief on her face. Her mouth hung open as she stared at me for a minute or so before she collected herself enough to continue.

"We were in this big hallway that led straight into some kind of holding cell. We found a computer next to the door, and 'Smalls' managed to get it to open our enclosure.

At this point I kind of realized that we were discovering something much more important than climbing a mountain, we were discovering something that was going to change the world. Either that, or we stumbled upon some secret government prison."

"Well, technically you were half right on both counts."

"What do you mean?"

"Well, it will change the world, but you can't tell anyone about it and by the time we finish in there, it is a prison for those things. That is why we need you to please explain exactly why, when we scanned the mountain, we discovered the life signs of several creatures inside, fully activated"

Her face dropped as if she knew they messed up.

"We released them by accident trying to open a door."

"Care to elaborate?"

She sat quietly for a few minutes like she was trying to piece together the whole situation.

"When we found those containers, we were terrified by what they held. Things we couldn't even dream of in our darkest nightmares. The containers all had these strange liquid-filled sacks above them and..."

"We are aware of the sacks. What I need to know is how did you activate the machines?"

She again sighed in annoyance before continuing on.

"We were trying to get out. Smalls was on one of the terminals and he was frantically trying to find an exit button when we heard a siren of some sort that chilled us to the bone. It was like nothing we'd ever heard in our lives, like a howling of wind mixed with an air raid siren. Then the room roared to life. The sacks just started draining through all the tubes and next thing we knew we heard loud thuds. We were all looking at each other, and then we moved, following the thumping noises. The creature we found looked like a mix of a worm and a dragon. It had fly-like wings attached to a slender scale-covered body. Its head looked like an earthworm engorging with fluids before letting out this horrendous growl that was so deep it shook the whole room. It wasn't long until we heard others waking up, and we started to run."

"We made it to a door, but the howls became so loud we couldn't even hear each other speak. That's when we *did* hear something familiar: the sound of glass shattering. The creatures weren't howling in pain; they were trying to escape."

"Smalls was able to get another door open, but when we passed through and closed it, we noticed that we were missing Samantha. With all the noise distracting us, one of those things must have grabbed her. It wasn't long before we heard those monsters screaming on the other side of the door and beating on it, trying to get through. Garry started shouting about how we had to turn back and open the door in case she was still alive, but we all knew she was gone. He charged at the computer and shoved Smalls and his girlfriend out of the way like they were nothing. I... I didn't have a choice. I still had my climbing hook and I swung."

"So you were the one to kill Garry?"

"I didn't want to! I had no choice! If I hadn't done what I did, he might have opened the door, dooming us all. Or worse: he might have released something else into the room we were in."

She'd risen abruptly, having kicked the chair back. She was poised like she was ready to jump over the table at me if she could. Almost as if her retelling was making her act out the events all over again. I made a note that medication might need to be administered.

"So yes, I killed him. It wasn't avoidable and I would do it again if I had to. I saved us!"

She sat back down in her chair with a fire in her eyes, the look of someone that fully believed in her conviction, as she paused. I spoke up to prod her to continue.

"Was that why you were avoiding telling us what happened?"

Looking up with tears in her eyes it seemed that this was what she was worried about.

"Yes, please don't arrest me for my actions. I didn't know what else to do and..."

"Ma'am, you are not in trouble. This conversation will be treated as if it never happened, and nothing will leave this room. Please continue," I lied.

A few more minutes passed as she collected herself again before continuing.

"When the shock of what I had just done wore off I found myself alone. Smalls and his girlfriend were gone. I was left alone in the dark."

"When the blood stopped thumping in my ears and the world came back from my tunnel vision, I turned on my headlamp and could see the dents forming in the door from the repeated abuse. I didn't know what else to do so I just ran. I ran as hard and as fast as I could. Making my way through the maze of giant tubes, I finally saw a light as the doors opened on the other side of the room. I saw someone run through them, and I was sure that it was my only way out. It led to a hallway and eventually some kind of elevator. There was no sign of Smalls or his girlfriend, so I boarded it and hit a random floor. When the doors opened, I was on a floor with a bunch of plant life. I was able to eventually find a pathway out like the one we came in on."

"So you managed to just happen to stumble across an exit?"

"How else was I supposed to have found it? Not like I had a freaking map."

"Again ma'am, I am only trying to get the facts straight."

"Well after I found my path, I climbed down to the way we used to get in and that was when I found Smalls. He was on his way out when one of those dragon things flew out of somewhere and used some kind of a sonic blast to shatter his body. I jumped down from where I was and drove my climbing pick into its head and fell to the ledge. I dragged him out of that hell hole, and that creature howled again, caving in the entryway."

"So after you dragged him off the mountain, we found you?"

"Yes."

"Okay then. I'll have one of our agents escort you back to your room and we will let you know when you are free to go."

As I was stacking my paperwork and collecting the tape recorder, she stopped me.

"Is... is Smalls going to be okay?"

I had a feeling there was more to this story than she was letting on, but I didn't want to risk anything being changed.

"We don't know yet. His injuries were quite severe and we just don't know if he will make it through the night."

I was lying to her; his injuries, although bad, were not life-threatening. He'd only broken a few bones and ruptured a lung and his eardrums. He also might be on something else to help with the internal bleeding, but the doctors expect a full recovery, more or less.

Heading out the door, my earpiece beeped, and I was notified that Smalls was just finishing up his version. All I had to do now was compare the stories. If all checked out, we should be good to go. I knew there was a way in, and we had more than enough firepower to take out the wounded creature. There was an exit with a relatively straight shot to it. I informed security to keep a close eye on our female guest in the meantime.

Walking down the hallway, I couldn't help but feel that we were wasting valuable time, and going off Ms. Bigs and her reaction to the 'multiple creatures' comment, I knew there had to be more than one of those creatures flying around in there. From the sound of it, however, these were going to be worse than the bat mummifier creatures from the last place. Those things were crazy: spiders the size of a horse with bat wings. They killed in the same manner as all the others though. They would grab one of my guys and wrap their legs around before it dug in and drained every ounce of liquid out of them. It was like watching a kid drain every last drop out of a juice box and then discard it to the side. I had seen too many soldiers kill their own just so they didn't have to die that way. "Mummify or mercy" – that is the only option we found once one of them gets you.

My intercom beeped and the familiar voice chimed in. "We are staged at the collapsed entrance. We are preparing the excavators and should be in within the hour."

"Copy that, proceed with caution, at least one dragon is flying around in there and from what Bigs told me, it's likely that there are others either still in containment or loose."

"Dragon, sir?"

"That's how she described it, dragon, fly wings, scaly worm-like body with sonic based defenses. Be advised that sonic blasts are strong enough to rupture organs and shatter bone."

"So you're saying ear plugs won't cut it this time?"

"Affirmative. Use of explosive rounds are authorized, as well as incendiary. Be safe and let me know when you get through. Over."

"Copy that, over and out."

I knew that it wasn't required for them to check in before entering, but once they were inside, we would have zero contact and I wouldn't see them again for years. Some I'll never see again. What I didn't understand though was that the things she'd described didn't seem like the other creatures. These monsters seemed to be strictly combat based.

Because we knew the risks of the last few facilities, we'd started our own unofficial tradition so that the fallen and survivors would always be remembered. The containment teams and I all would open coms and we would share a song about the end of the world as an inside joke, but also so that they understood that the mission must succeed at all costs. We'd share a shot and the mission commences.

I was lost in thought when one of the interns ran up to me with a file. "Sir, I have the deposition from Smalls."

"Thank you, was there anything else?"

Timidly, he pulled out another piece of paper and handed it to me.

"He asked for me that someone with the authority to handle this make sure that the other survivor has no contact with him."

"Well, that seems kind of an odd request, given that she saved him, at least according to her story."

Opening the note, I only had to read the first few lines in order to understand.

"She is not who she says she is, she kidnapped my group and forced us up that mountain. She held us at gunpoint and used us as bait to access one of the computers inside."

I'd suspected as I'd listened to her that her story wasn't fully true and seemed way too convenient. By the time I got down to the holding cells the guard was already dead and she was gone.

"Fuck!"

I just knew this was going to be a long night. Grabbing the closest phone, I put out an emergency alert. "Attention all staff and security. We have a spy in the building. Be advised, the suspect is six foot two, female, large athletic build, brunette, brown eyes. She is potentially armed and dangerous. Medical, I need you in holding cell three!"

It didn't take long to find her once the security footage was re-watched. It turns out I had shown up right after she had killed her guard. She was still in the room and wasn't too far from the very phone I was using. We found her huddled in a cupboard. Now I was forced to find out the truth... by any means necessary.

I sat at my desk with the other survivors' files and it seemed clear that pretty much everything she told me Smalls did, she had forced him to do. She had stalked them at the hostel where they'd been staying and found out their backgrounds from the conversations.

She'd beaten Samantha to death in order to make the others listen and prove a point. She then slashed Smalls' girlfriend's ankle with the same climbing hook that she would later use to kill Garry. The creature then engulfed the girlfriend into its mouth and spit out a dried husk.

The only reason Smalls had survived was because he managed to get free the same way they came in. He'd had to jump, and as he was falling the creature had blasted him with a sonic wave. He was almost free but then she'd escaped a few hours after him. He had crawled to the road where we found them, and she was about to finish the job and kill him when we showed up.

The only thing I could figure for that timing was that they must have escaped literal seconds between each other in our time.

It was just a matter of time before we knew who she was working for. I might not approve of the methods used to get her to talk, but if there is a competitor, then we need to know what their intentions are.

"These time dilations are insane." I said aloud, though no one was there to hear my observation.

My earpiece beeped again.

"Hey buddy, we just broke through and killed two contacts inside the wall. We are outside the entryway now awaiting orders."

Opening up the drawer of my desk I pulled out my now half empty bottle and poured a shot.

"Attention all units, open coms"

As the song finished playing, we all took our drinks, the alcohol's burn fueling our need to succeed.

After this mission wrapped up, we took our samples and after a few years of the eggheads doing their thing, they discovered that the facility was much like the smaller one we'd found in Iraq. The smaller construct as well as the one in the mountain appeared to be... growing like some kind of

metallic organic crystal.

Recording: 009 - File- 2- Code Name "The Sea of Terror"

(T- minus two hours before impact)

Going through my older reports I came across my first real challenge file. It was only a few months after the mountain incident and I was being recognized by the higher-ups for my ability to get these jobs done.

Picking up the older file, I felt a surge of memories flood in from the cluster fuck that was this mission. Not only was it extremely difficult, but we found ourselves facing the facilities defense mechanisms that were now sporadically popping up, almost as if they were anticipating us now.

Case# 009

Location: Baltic sea

Special procedures:

- Use of EMP shielded equipment only.

- All dive equipment must have an analog backup source for oxygen.

- All personnel are to be trained in underwater combat and survival.

- Communication within 200 yards of the entryway is not possible, must be fluent with sign language.

Cover story: Area is to be secured and cordoned off as a boating Hazard. Buoys with warnings of methane gas are to be distributed in a 10-mile radius from ground zero. Any reports of the escaped creatures are to be followed and all creatures recovered or neutralized. Depth charges are to be used to keep "BIG BLUE" contained.

During an underwater survey for places to drill offshore oil wells, an anomaly had been discovered. Something alien-shaped was located on the ocean floor. There appeared to be a sliding path to the anomaly, however we later determined that that happened to be a loading or an unloading ramp for whoever built this particular facility.

We discovered this due to the escape of Big Blue. According to the camera footage shot during the mission, the whole building extended down miles into the earth's crust and contained several very large holding chambers. One of them housed Big Blue in stasis until it was activated for unknown reasons. They also contained several smaller creatures resembling disturbing mermaids of all things.

Taking out the old VHS tapes, I felt compelled to watch them out of nostalgia's sake. But I knew that time was not on my side. I understood that, at any point, an escape or full release could potentially end a significant amount of life on the planet before we could contain it, simply by decimating the ocean's ecosystem.

This was quite possibly going to be one of the last things that I could guarantee was recorded., Indeed, it could be one of the last things I may *ever* do.

I could feel the dust that had collected on it as I opened the clam-shelled case and slid the tape into the VCR. It made its loud clunking as it set into place and I pressed play.

The video started by showing the slow descent of the small submarine into the affected area. For all the advanced technology we had at our disposal, including stuff that wasn't even available for military application yet, it meant nothing once we entered into the dead zone.

The submarine carried the squad down as far as it was capable of going, and then the team launched via personal-sized torpedo-like vehicles that split apart when within range of the facility entrance.

I had been given command when my predecessor decided to paint the wall with a bullet. According to his note, he couldn't live with the knowledge or the pressure anymore; of knowing that at any point one of these places could wake up and release whatever hell it contained. So I got a promotion, and unfortunately I also got his old office. Admittedly, it had a better view, but they left the bullet hole as a reminder of the importance of the position.

Watching the video feed switch to their shoulder mounted cameras, I remember having to document their approach. When they switched over to their tanks instead of rebreathers. When they had to get their analog gear transferred. When they attached the more tech-reliant equipment used to get there to floaters and sent it back to the surface.

I had to be sure all rules were followed as they located the entrance. When the scanner activated and the door opened, the camera feed was transferred to a cut-together mix of the different perspectives, almost like it was a movie. This was done as a precaution so if word did get out, or if a copy was stolen, we would be able to play it off as just an independent film from an unknown production company.

As soon as the door closed, the water was instantly drained from the facility and the squad found themselves in the ever-familiar hallway.

For as many different variations I have seen of these places by now, they all had the same type of entry layout. it was as if the entryways were some mass-produced components that simply attached to the different environmental containment constructs. If it wasn't so terrifying, I would be beyond impressed.

The team entered the facility fully armed and ready. I had been briefed that a team had already previously been dispatched to the location; however, none of the members were ever recovered and from what scans we could get, they showed that they had failed in their mission to destroy the life support system and the main computer rooms.

The footage went as usual until the shooting started. It turned out that this facility had a unique security system in the form of several man-sized versions of the creatures from the desert which roamed the spaces and flooded areas where their mermaid counterparts laid in wait. There must have been some sort of an alert sent out from the previous arks being shut down and an emergency security response had been activated in the remaining constructs.

Granted, we had only located thirty others at that point, but after all these years, it was more than enough for me to be worried about. We had other ongoing missions in those locations; however, due to the time dilation, we had still not made contact with those teams to find out if they were successful or not. If we continued doing these missions as we were, we may have risked an automatic response of mass release and we don't even know how many are left.

~

Leaning back in my chair as the video continued to play, I understood better now that I was relying on this structure's resilience. If I knew then what I know now, we should have just left them alone. Because at least then we were ignorant and could have just lived out our pitiful existence never knowing some forgotten race of precursors had saved us until we went and fucked it all up.

The creatures were fast, but not faster than the weapons my soldiers were carrying. Even so, the creatures were able to take out one of the squad members. The rest, after securing the area, collected his gear and placed the man's body at the entryway where they had entered in order to collect it later. After they completed their impromptu service for the fallen comrade, they continued on with the mission.

For some reason this location had a different layout and the server room was very deep into the building. There was a strange void in the floor plan, as if it had been where it was supposed to be, but had moved in order to protect itself.

The cameras switched between each other as they cleared the floor of any hostiles and found one of the time distortion elevators. When they all hopped down the video glitched, but was not as affected as we thought it would be. As they descended in the elevator, they entered a section open to one of the larger holding cells. What was housed there was something that could only be classified as a leviathan. It dwarfed a blue whale even though it shared several features as far as body shape. Its head was a mass of tentacles in the same configurations as the giants in the desert with the arms. Each one ended in a beak-like appendage with a gullet full of hollow teeth. The eyes were like giant satellite dishes, black and inky with all the warmth of a doll's unending gaze. This thing was clearly designed to be the ultimate apex predator of the ocean.

This was the first time any of us had met or seen "Big Blue". What we didn't know was that it was awake and watching. We thought that it was still in its stasis phase, contained, dormant and still harmless.

Until its tentacles started to stretch out from its now opening maw revealing even more teeth the size of cars.

It didn't take long for the agents to realize the creature was alive and well. Guess we should be thanking the creators of these places for building a strong enough elevator because once it realized that they knew it was alive and not dormant, it attacked the shaft like a shark in a feeding frenzy. Its beak-tipped tentacles wrapped around the elevator itself and began pulling and thrashing with an ungodly power. The men were clearly worried; however, they knew that this place had been designed to hold these creatures.

They eventually made it to the lower level where the mainframe was located and as soon as the door opened the video erupted with gunfire as a small horde of those smaller vampire-like things began to swarm in. In the firefight two more agents were lost as the creatures wrapped their bodies around them and then squeezed on whatever limb they happened to be attached to. I heard the muffled screams becoming dry and soon the bones shattered. The other managed to pull the trigger of his weapon, spraying bullets from within, killing himself and the creature holding him.

The whole engagement only took a matter of thirty seconds, but the chaos and damage done looked like a slaughterhouse. When the dust settled there were only two agents left. They spoke to each other and continued on to strip the needed ammunition and explosives from their fallen friends.

~

I gripped the arms of my chair knowing what was coming. I remember as if it was happening right now.

~

What they had discussed was a suicide run. The one pulled up a crudely drawn map and marked three checkpoints. The other loaded up on ammo and they began their final run to their goal.

At every corner they just started blind-firing and fighting through everything that got in their way. The flashes obscured a lot of what was happening as the camera jerked around. The video switched to a man strapped with explosives, his camera whipping around when his guard was ripped away from his side. He turned and ran faster until he reached the door, pounding the proper sequence of buttons into the keypad, and the door began to open. The video turned back then, showing a creature different from the others.

Its body was a roughly human-shaped torso with whip-thin appendages draped to its sides, each with some kind of bone blades tipping them. Its three thin legs twitched as one of the appendages shot forward, and a soldier fell to the ground, the hook-like blade lodged itself deep into the calf. Then came the horror. It began slamming him against the walls of the hallway. With each hit, the camera would glitch until it finally fell free and showed the soldier thrown away from the creature, back into the server room. A burst of bullets scattered the wall with holes and the ink black blood of the creature before it fell dead in front of the camera.

Someone grabbed the still-recording camera and limped back into the room. The soldier with explosives was writhing in pain on the floor. The still-standing team member knelt down and offered to plant the bombs and carry his comrade out, but the soldier pushed him away. The man pulled out a medical kit and stuck two syringes into the dying man. I later found out that he was the team medic, and that it was morphine with an adrenaline chaser. The medic rose, grabbed as much gear as he could carry, and began to run.

A sharp jerk and the dull thud of an explosion shook the elevator as it ascended upward. . What equated to emergency power was activated, and our surviving team member made it to the exit. He'd collected all the cameras on the way out: he knew their importance.

Sadly he did not make it to the surface. He was able to get his suit on and breathing apparatus secured and when the room filled so he could swim out. It turns out that the detonation had somehow activated the hidden exit just outside the entry. We can only speculate as to what happened to him, because the camera was turned off and he'd managed to send it to the surface via a floater beacon. By the time we'd recovered the tapes, Big Blue had already started attacking our ships. I watched in horror as our men and women were just snatched off the sides of the boats as the larger tentacles began carving through hulls like they were butter. We'd fought the monster for a solid hour, blasting chunks out of it with naval artillery and torpedoes until it finally sank down to the bottom of the ocean.

~

Just thinking about what had happened, how close I and the rest of my team had come to death, sent shivers down my spine, even now.

~

We weren't able to kill the beast, but we did deal enough damage for it to go back down to the floor. We had managed to destroy its main flipper-like arms and it could no longer stay afloat. However once it hit the sea's floor, its abdomen split open and unfurled into a series of lobster-like legs, and its once-blubbery skin then had some kind of hardened shell, almost as if it was a soft shell crab after molting when we were fighting it. This information was gleaned from a submarine video feed.

Since that day, even though we don't have any way to currently kill it, we do have it contained using specially built depth charges and electrified mines just outside the dead zone. What worries us is that there may be other sub-oceanic facilities. Back in 1997, it emitted a subsonic call that was picked up all around the world, and we started seeing an increase in strange activity surrounding other known, and at the time unknown, locations.

That was the day we knew the world was ending.

~

Ejecting the tape from the player, I understood that the last words on that recording were far truer now than I'd ever thought they could be.

File 3- Code Name "The Pass"

(T-minus one hour before impact. All personnel report to designated pods.)

Taking a swig from my little glass buddy here, I continued through these files. The once-burning amber liquid was barely a tangy tingle as it drained down my gullet. Even with the final timer counting down, I just felt like reminiscing on the last few years. I guess I just want to feel like maybe I had actually made a difference. Well at least I thought I did and, as they say, it's the thought that counts.

Right? At least that's what I told myself as I downed the rest of the glass.

"Oh here's a good one!" I thumb through the old folders.

Pouring myself another glass I opened it up and paced the room.

~

Case #015

Location: Russia

Special containment:

- Use lead lined containers for all transportation of specimens out of this area.

- Any and all escaped creatures are to be terminated on sight.

- Death squads are to patrol the known perimeter every hour.

- Any and all remains are to be processed down and stored in lead lined barrels for proper radioactive disposal.

- Cover story: Area is deemed unsafe and an avalanche hazard. The radioactive signatures are remnants of old soviet nuclear testing. If asked the barrels simply contain hazardous materials off to be disposed of.

~

Now, what happened to those kids was horrible. We had just started running into creatures meant for military grade engagements. These were weapons meant to kill on a drastic scale and to poison the land for centuries. Deadly for us, but to them nothing more than a few years of extra sleep as the world regrew. I still to this day cannot wrap my mind around just how old these beings were.

When we'd deciphered what we could from the inscriptions and hieroglyphs, it turned out that the outsides of each facility were different. They each had their own stories that depicted the particular facility's times being activated, and in doing so that single facility caused who knows how many extinctions itself, because our sorry asses couldn't get close enough to it. Shit made Chernobyl look like a sunburn.

Whoever was making these places were seriously not fucking around. I mean seriously the amount of radiation some of these things were generating were half as high as a freshly detonated nuke.

The strangest part was that when this one activated, it had a minimum of twenty separate events. We only knew this because we happened to come across a record of it in another facility that it had helped in the past. That would make this one a minimum of seventy to eighty billion fucking years old. Which seems completely impossible given the age of the earth, and the Big Bang was only around fourteen billion years ago.

The only theories anyone could ever come up with was either they were alien constructs placed here and are therefore older than our planet and our known existence of everything, or what we are dealing with were from a different far more ancient dimension. Which shockingly enough is kinda the truth. The funniest part is I know the answer to this question now and I wish I didn't.

As I held the folder open, I skimmed through the boring prep work and got to the good parts. I was running out of time anyways and I was way too drunk at this point to give a solid shit.

~

We had just spent a week hiking and carrying all our equipment up the mountain to set up our forward operating base. It didn't take long for us to be attacked. It was almost as if the things were waiting for us. We started seeing bumps in the snow rise up into little dunes only a few feet tall but very wide.

As soon as we activated our radiation detectors they started going off with an unlivable amount of radiation unless we moved then and there to a less contaminated area. Problem was, whatever was causing the spikes was following us.

We must have climbed and moved around for hours; the whole time we worried that the thunder that had come out of nowhere was going to cause an avalanche. It was so powerful it shook the very ground we stood on. We found out that it wasn't thunder though. God help us all.

I remember we were near a possible fall zone when I turned around to tell the rest of the team to watch their step. I saw one of the dunes moving behind one of the faceless team members.

He didn't have a chance. The creature erupted from its hiding place and in an instant he was gone, like a magician just abracadabra-ed his ass into oblivion. All hell broke loose and the snow almost seemed to reverse back into the air with the flurry of those creatures springing to life. Their bodies were heavily armored with thick leather like hides, a heavy coat of white hair and so many teeth and claws. It looked like a giant, violent, hairy millipede from hell. They tunneled through the snow with ease. It took several risky shots with a grenade launcher and the death of a good soldier to stop the assault.

This thing wasn't a creature for harvesting, this was a fuck-you to nature and anything else that got in the way.

We later discovered that there were tunnels leading up from this facility, but due to the radioactive nature of the place and the fact that it would be certain death for anyone going in, the call was made to fill every hole we found with concrete and molten lead in an effort to try to shield what we could. Cobalt plugs were also made and sunk into the lead as it solidified making the tightest seal possible.

I didn't really care what anyone said. I didn't think *anything* was tearing through that much metal. But the call was made, seeing as how we couldn't even get in there to see what horrors this facility housed. Quite frankly, if what we had just fought was a small one from the facility, the bigger ones were a definite no-no for us to attempt to deal with.

~

We spent so much time in the aftermath just trying to dispose of the bodies and radioactive snow that we eventually just cordoned the entire area off.

I realize that I am speeding through these files now. But I want there to be some sort of record if this world survives. Even if we don't, maybe somehow in the future when man (or whatever replaces humans) evolves again someone will come across this time capsule and these records, and hopefully they will help.

Final Report

I poured the last of my bottle and swished it around the glass. I knew that I had no more time to waste and that it was time to make my final, final report. Grabbing my computer and as many files as possible, I made my way to the "safe" room, closed the door, and overrode the security measures to lock it down indefinitely. Granted, that means that whoever finds this will have to possess a level of technology high enough to cut through this much steel and various alloys. But it also meant that those fuckers outside destroying the planet and slaughtering humanity can't get in either.

I had spent the last few days stockpiling all the weapons and various computers that I could along with just as many power sources so that, if someone does get in, they can at least attempt to gain access to this information. I was also able to bring a few examples of the creatures for study if and when someone discovers this.

I made it pretty clear how to open this box from the outside, so hopefully whoever finds it can read English, or has the technology and knowledge to be able to decode or translate it. I set up my computer and the now all too familiar report page and began typing.

Case# 037

Location: Earth/ Moon

special containment: No way in hell

Cover Story: freaking None

This file is to be reviewed by anyone who happens to find this capsule. My only hope is that you find this before your timer is up and you spend the remainder of your time preparing. Please bear with me as I am very drunk.

Contained in a separate file there will be a list of all known locations and possible places of interest. Again, I apologize for any possible inaccuracies in the information, given that we still don't know what happens when they finish...

(burp)...

...erasing us from this world, but I want you or whoever finds this to know that we fought to the very end and we did destroy a fair number of their facilities. In the end, though, we just could not defend against what's coming. Even nuking the moon wasn't enough. Yes, that's right – we nuked the goddamn moon. The facilities still opened and the cosmic horror of what was truly inside of it – we just didn't have the weaponry to defend against it.

Up until this point we had a ninety-five percent success rate in either destroying or decommissioning the facilities through various means. We did the best we could. However just because we failed doesn't mean that you will.

In the same file that contains the locations of the constructs you will also find everything needed to set up manufacturing for the level of weaponry we have at our current time, as well as for weapons systems that we had in development.

In this room, you will find useful information, as well as some of the armaments I was able to procure. Please use them well and do not use them on each other. We spent so much time fighting each other that we failed to progress to become a society that could stand strong against any and all trials. So hopefully y'all aren't fuck ups like us.

This file will consist of all the information we were able to gather, well, at least an abridged version, given that my current time is weaning away.

The origins of these creatures are far beyond just our space and time. They are from a parallel universe, from what we were able to determine.

They have always... been. Long before our world became inhabitable, before it even became a planet – even before the Big Bang created our universe. When we discovered the first of their facilities, we learned how to control it and, at a substantial price, we cleared out all of the ghastly inhabitants. That is when we believe the SOS went out, and they decided it was time to punish us. To end us. The facilities began to activate. We discovered that all of these facilities, except for a choice few, descend deep into the planet's core. Those that weren't embedded balls deep were actually seeds of sorts that would eventually grow and create new branches, if you will.

The core isn't even the molten ball of iron we thought it was. It was solid. Like the core of a golf ball.

When we sent a team down there, it appeared to function bio-mechanically as we explored deeper. The heat we registered outside the construct was beyond anything that should have allowed for any living being yet inside it was only a mere eighty- five degrees within, if that.

What we discovered was that each facility was an extension of this massive cybernetic creature. All the extinction level events we were seeing on the walls, those were just its feeding times. We survived because the baby skipped a damn bottle.

Upon this revelation we also now understood that we were destined to be its nutrients. That the facilities' release was nothing more than that civilization's turn to be sacrificed. We were a literal self-sustaining egg.

Which brings me to the moon, and subsequently to other dead rocky planets in the known galaxy.

We discovered that the moon was hollow, or at least that it rang like it was hollow. We weren't the only ones to notice. We had a friend who worked for one of the world's space agencies and he also began monitoring it, but had no idea about the significance of his research.

Well since the moon was also an "egg" when it hatched it released something massive and at the same time … launched… (sorry slight baby burp there) … it launched a piece of its shell towards earth. I am currently awaiting its arrival.

The nearest we can figure is that when the big bang happened, it was basically two higher dimensions making a baby... or several babies. We have no clue how to fathom that with any laws of physics. However, that is the current theory and from what I've seen, it seems the most logical.

I kind of wish I had more to drink.

The nearest we can figure is that the galaxy was created as a nursery or womb. These eggs were formed here billions of years ago after being fertilized by whatever weird-assed thing decided to essentially stick its dick in a different universe.

Pardon my vulgarity, I've had a lot to drink. No sense in dying alone and sober.

The reason we kept getting older and older dates from inside is because every extinction event leads to a molting of the outer layers of the planet, and the organism itself for a short time, relatively speaking, just kind of floated around like a giant robot space infant, until its gravity pulled in a fresh amount of resources and created the next shell like casing for it to grow more and allow for the next level of civilizations or, as I'm gonna call it, the next feeding time, to evolve and come into being.

The smaller creatures as well as the larger ones were designed to drain all living creatures on the planet of any fluids. They would then bring that material to the respective facility for deposit. The reason we were seeing more weaponized creatures was because it was essentially an immune response in order to save the embryo.

If the moon's creature is anything to go by, our planet's being is much larger and by extension our ultimate demise will be much more explosive when it finally hatches. The tectonic plates are nothing more than the cracks starting to form... we saw the same situation unfold on the moon before the current predicament.

The piece of the lunar surface heading towards earth will be here in only a few more minutes. I... I don't know if I will survive. The estimated size of the shell is the size of Japan. The projected path puts it landing in the ocean; however, with the amount of force it is coming with, it is going to vaporize a significant percentage of the water, also causing who knows how much carnage with the tsunami that would engulf the coastal areas. The other concern is that without the moon and its gravitational pull, what is left of our oceans would be thrown into chaos, thus resulting in an altered... everything. Life as we know it would not survive. Hell, I don't even know if our other teams still inside the facilities will survive. they don't even have a clue what the fuck is going on out there.

I know what I am telling you... whoever you are, stranger – is something absolutely crazy and I know if or when you find these files, you will chalk it up to the ramblings of an insane lunatic. I know that the files and folders on this computer will more than answer any question, but I just have to do something to keep my mind preoccupied with...

~

The file ended abruptly and I was in such shock that not only had I discovered a previously unknown architecture, but found something so technologically advanced with what appeared to be a human inside.

The shielded area had the words "Open me" burned into it with some kind of torch and It took days to cut through the wall. We were horrified to find mummified remains of what the experts guessed were the creatures that the man on the recording was speaking of.

(audio recorder engaged)

We quickly secured the area and we have taken special care to not destroy the perfectly preserved bodies. We know the one is human, but the others appear to be some type of horrendous creatures. They have already been sent to our labs to be studied and categorized.

As of yet we are not sure how authentic this whole place is, but given its depth into the earth and the story I just read, I have no idea how anyone would or could afford to create such a hoax. However, his description mentions a tidally-locked moon, yet our planet has never had a moon to exert that kind of influence upon our oceans.

If what he says is true, then we must take great care and not get blood or anything wet near those monsters. The wealth of tools and technology that this society had is beyond anything we would hope to achieve.

It even explains the weird puzzle piece that is the rogue continent. All the others fit together except for Luna-ta.

If even half of this record is true then we may have a large problem on our hands, one that must be addressed sooner than later. I have a friend that deals with theoretical physics and is researching dimensional travel... our planet is already dying, I hope that he has a breakthrough soon. Maybe this is the technology he needs to help his research.

(audio recorder disengaged)

Made in the USA
Middletown, DE
31 March 2023